What a Wimp!

What a Wimp!

by CAROL CARRICK

Drawings by Donald Carrick

CLARION BOOKS

TICKNOR & FIELDS: A HOUGHTON MIFFLIN COMPANY

NEW YORK

For Mike Joyce, who would have helped

Clarion Books
Ticknor & Fields, a Houghton Mifflin Company
Text copyright © 1983 by Carol Carrick
Illustrations copyright © 1983 by Donald Carrick

Library of Congress Cataloging in Publication Data
Carrick, Carol.
    What a wimp!
    Summary: Although his teacher, mother, and
older brother are sympathetic, Barney knows
he'll have to find his own way to deal with
the bully, Lenny.
    [1. Bullies — Fiction] I. Carrick, Donald,
ill. II. Title.
PZ7.C2344Wh 1983   [Fic]   82-9597
ISBN 0-89919-139-8
A 10 9 8 7 6 5 4

Contents

1

A Crummy Start

The first time Lenny Coots bothered him, Barney didn't know who Lenny was. Barney hardly knew anyone in Hillside then.

After Barney's parents divorced, his mother decided to move them to Hillside. She had been happy spending her summers there as a little girl. "You'll love it!" she said. "It's the perfect place for a boy to grow up."

She had gotten Barney and his older brother, Russ, excited about moving to the country. They had told all the kids in their old school what a wonderful time they were going to have.

It snowed the first week after they moved in. Because Barney had lived in the city, he'd never had a sled before. His mother bought him one at the shopping center, and Barney took it to the big hill a few blocks from his house.

It was a terrific hill for sledding, and Barney had it all to himself that morning. The runners hissed over the snow as the sled went faster, faster, until it hit a scary bump in the middle. Then it dropped from under Barney for a second. If he kept his balance, he landed on the sled again and rode on down to the bottom of the hill.

So when the two strange boys appeared, Barney felt a pang of disappointment. Sledding would be more fun if he was with friends, but these boys were older, and he felt a little shy. Only one of them had a sled. The other boy, the one with almost white hair, was wearing the kind of shiny purple and gold athletic jacket Barney's brother had always wanted. The boy carried a broken branch shaped like a hockey stick, and he was swinging it at clumps of snow.

When Barney passed them on his way up the hill, he said, "Hi." That's the first thing he had learned about living in the country. People said hello even if they didn't know you. His mother said it was because country people were more friendly. At first it had surprised him, but now he was getting used to it.

The boys didn't answer right away. Then one of

them mumbled, "Hi," to Barney's back and they both snickered. That was when Barney began to feel uncomfortable.

The two of them were standing in the middle of the slope watching Barney as he prepared to start down again. He still hadn't gotten the courage to belly flop, so he was wishing they wouldn't look. Barney sat on the sled, pushed off with his feet, and held on to the rope for dear life.

Just as he passed them, the kid with the stick threw it in front of the sled. When the runners hit the stick, the sled stopped suddenly. Barney went flying in the air. He hit the ground hard — UNH! — and slid sideways down the hill.

Barney was so surprised he just lay there for a few seconds. Then he got up and brushed himself off, picking the snow out of his collar. The two boys were laughing. Barney kept his head down so they couldn't see by his face that he was upset.

"Hey, kid! Can I use your sled?"

Barney didn't realize at first that the boy was talking to him. It was the blond one, the one who had thrown the stick. He was holding Barney's sled. Barney thought maybe he was kidding. Did he really think Barney would want to lend him his sled now?

And why couldn't he use his friend's? But Barney didn't know how to say no. Maybe the boy really hadn't meant to hurt Barney. Maybe he meant it as a joke. His brother, Russ, always told Barney he should be a better sport.

Reluctantly, Barney nodded.

The boy yelled to his friend, "Hey, Caruso! Wait up!" The two of them ran to the top and made a running bellyflop down the hill.

Barney thought he would get the sled back after one or two turns, but the boy took no notice of him standing at the top of the hill. After the third time, Barney got up the courage to ask. "Could I have my sled back now?"

The boy did another bellyflop and yelled back over his shoulder, "Just one more time."

The two boys were having a race, trying to cut each other off, and making a point of piling up at the bottom. Barney had to admit it looked like fun. He wished they'd ask him to join in. He was getting cold just standing there, especially his toes. A lot of the snow had gotten down his jacket and was melting there. The other boys seemed to be getting bored with sledding. The idea now was to crash into each other as much as possible, and with Barney's new sled. He

waited till they came back up to the top of the hill.

"I want my sled. *Now!*" he said.

"Once more," the blond boy promised, getting ready to slide down again.

"No! You said that before."

"Just once. Just one time," the boy said, holding up one finger and faking a really sincere expression.

Barney knew better by this time.

"I want it now! NOW!" he yelled angrily. But he didn't think he really had a chance of getting the sled back. There were two of them, and they were at least two years older than he was.

"Oh, here then. Take it," the boy said, sounding disgusted. He gave the sled a shove. It went speeding down the hill. The other boy giggled.

Barney trotted after the sled, slipping in the snow and feeling foolish.

"What a wimp!" the blond one muttered.

Barney was almost to the bottom when he heard the roar of their sled right behind him. He jumped aside as they careened past. Riding double-decker, they came as close as possible to hitting him, then stopped by tipping over at the bottom of the hill.

Barney picked up the rope on his sled and dragged it toward the road.

"Going home?" the blond kid sang out.

Barney didn't answer.

"I thought you were in a big hurry to use your sled," called Caruso.

Barney pretended to ignore them.

One of them said something too low for Barney to hear. The other laughed.

Hot tears of rage spilled down Barney's frozen cheeks. He brushed them quickly away. The icy mitten left his face stinging. What a crummy way to start off in a new town.

2

Some Fun!

When Barney came into the living room, Russ was watching wrestling on television. His mother was on her way upstairs with a carton of books. They had been living in the Hillside house for two weeks, but everything wasn't unpacked yet.

"How did the sled work?" his mother stopped on the stairs to ask.

"Fine," answered Barney.

"You don't sound that way."

"It was fun. I'm just cold," Barney explained. He was ashamed to tell her he had come home because of the two boys, especially in front of Russ. His brother would say he shouldn't have let them bother him.

It must have been after lunchtime. A sandwich and

an oatmeal cookie were left for him next to Russ's empty plate on the coffee table. Barney took a bite of his sandwich and looked at the screen. A man with frizzy bleached hair and with a roll of flab drooping over his tights was sitting on the back of another wrestler. The one on the bottom looked pretty normal. Barney decided he must be the good guy. He pounded on the floor with both hands while the man on top was twisting his foot off.

"Isn't there anything else on?" Barney asked.

"I want to watch this," Russ answered.

"Aww." Barney went in the kitchen and poured himself a glass of milk. When he came back, he saw that his cookie was gone.

"Russ!"

"What?"

"My cookie."

"What about your cookie?"

"You took it."

"No, I didn't," said Russ, trying to look innocent, but he started to laugh.

"Come on," said Barney, laughing, too. He jumped on Russ and shoved his hand between the couch cushions to feel for the cookie. "Where did you put it?"

"I don't have it," protested Russ. "I swear." But he was still laughing.

Barney's mother came downstairs with the emptied carton.

"Mom, Russ took my cookie," Barney complained.

"Then get another one," his mother said. "And bring your plate back to the kitchen. Russ's, too."

"Why do I have to bring his?" grumbled Barney.

"Because I asked you to," said his mother as she disappeared down the basement stairs. Russ made a face at him.

Barney came back with another cookie and sat down on the couch. The frizzy-haired wrestler must have won, because two tag teams were getting their instructions from the referee.

"Oooo! Cookie!" said Russ. "Cookie Monster love cookie!" He tried to snatch Barney's cookie.

"Knock it off!" Barney protested.

Russ grabbed him by the shoulders, but Barney hunched over and stuffed the cookie in his mouth. Russ began to tickle his ribs. Barney was very ticklish. He broke out in giggles, spraying cookie crumbs all over the couch.

Russ rolled him over and sat on his stomach, pinning his wrists. Then Russ started bouncing on him.

Barney laughed, and what remained of the cookie drooled out of the corners of his mouth.

"Oh, gross!" said Russ with mock disgust. He moved off.

"You dumbhead!" said Barney, getting up and wiping his face with his sleeve.

"What! Are you challenging the champ?" Russ asked, and he locked Barney's neck in the crook of his arm. "The champ has him in a headlock, folks," he said, imitating the voice of a sports announcer. "Now the champ switches to his specialty hold. The crowd is going wild. YAY!"

"Ow, ow! That hurts!" said Barney. "Let go!"

"Not until you give up," Russ bargained.

"I give up! I give up!" Barney agreed right away. "I said I give up!"

Russ let him go.

"You jerk!" yelled Barney, angrily rubbing his shoulder. "That hurts!"

"Aw, c'mon. It didn't hurt that much. We were just having fun."

"What *you* call fun," Barney said, and he kicked Russ in the shin.

"So!" Russ grinned wickedly. "You haven't given up after all."

He grabbed Barney's arm and pulled him down on the couch. Just then their mother came up from the basement with another carton.

"Mom," Barney whined, "Russ is beating up on me."

"Russ, will you please stop that," she said, looking annoyed. "You're thirteen years old. It's about time you were a little help to me — both of you."

She glared at them and then added. "It looks as though you need something to occupy yourselves. Come down to the basement with me and I'll give you some boxes to carry upstairs."

"But I'm watching this program," Russ protested.

"It doesn't look like that to me," his mother said.

Russ switched off the set. As he followed Barney, he gave him a shove. "See what you did, tattletale."

"What *I* did!" Barney answered. "It's *your* fault. You're always picking on me."

It was true, thought Barney as he clumped down the basement stairs. Russ had started it. It was just like sledding this morning. He was having a great time till those other kids came. Why couldn't they all just leave him alone?

3

Hermie

The new school was not going so well for Barney, either.

His old school had been fun. Barney's class had spent a lot of time sitting on the rug with Miss Rose, their teacher, and discussing things. Only they didn't call her Miss Rose, they called her Debbie. Barney thought Debbie was beautiful, even though she wore a lot of makeup, and he knew she thought he was special, too. He was always the one who helped the others with their problems.

Problem number one for Barney now was Mrs. Bemouth, the fourth-grade teacher. Mrs. Bemouth said her name was pronounced Bi-muth and rhymed with

Plymouth. Barney thought her name should rhyme with *mammoth* because she was as big as a woolly mammoth, and just about as ancient.

Mrs. Bemouth's hair was a pale, pinkish color that didn't look real. It was like the fake hair on his cousin's doll. Barney thought it was a wig, but his mother said it just wasn't the teacher's real color.

From the start Barney was positive that Mrs. Bemouth didn't like him. For one thing, she never pinned up his papers with the special ones the way Debbie had in his old school. Instead, they came back marked with warnings like "Watch your margins!" or "Neatness!" And when they practiced letter writing, he had to do his over if it had too many mistakes. So now he only used words he knew how to spell.

Debbie always said that what you wrote was more important than how you wrote it. Correct spelling and punctuation would come later. But Mrs. Bemouth said it was important to form only good habits. She pinned up poems like the ones Marybeth Norton wrote. Marybeth's were written in perfect script, decorated with yellow suns and rows of flowers.

After recess on Monday morning, Mrs. Bemouth told the class to get out their math workbooks and solve the problems on pages 26 through 28. Ugh!

thought Barney when he opened his book. The heading on page 26 was MULTIPLICATION WITH TWO DIGITS.

Mrs. Bemouth expected him to know everything the rest of the class had learned. She acted as if it were his fault that he hadn't been in her class from the beginning of the year.

Barney did all right with math except for multiplication. In the other school they had just started learning their times tables, so he was a little behind this class. He had trouble carrying. He couldn't remember whether he should add the number he carried before or after he multiplied the number in the next column.

Barney did the first three and a half problems on page 26. Then he turned the page to see how many problems were on the next two pages. He groaned. There were three rows to do on both pages. He looked around the room. It was quiet except for an occasional sigh from someone else who was having trouble.

Barney went back to the problem he was working on: 26×14. "Six times four is . . ." He couldn't remember. "Six times three is eighteen, and another six would make . . ." He had to count it out on his fingers. "Twenty-four," he figured. He put down the 4 and carried the 2. "But now what do I do with the two?" he wondered. He checked the first problem to see what he had done there: 3×4. That would be 12. He knew his three times tables. But then why had he written a 7?

"Maybe I added by mistake," he thought. He erased the 7, but the eraser on his pencil was dried up. It made a black streak on the paper. Could he have added the other problems, too? He checked them. Yes, they *were* wrong. He began to erase the mistakes, but it made the page all messy.

Barney stared at the rows of numbers. Now he was really mixed up. His head started to ache. He propped his elbow on the desk and rested his head in his right hand. Then he noticed his left hand curled at the top of the notebook. It reminded him of the hand puppets Debbie had shown them how to make.

With his ballpoint pen he drew two black dots on the thumb side of his first finger, near the base. He made a circle around each dot for eyes, with slanting eyebrows over them. He bent his thumb and hooked his finger around his thumbnail. His thumb became the lower jaw forming a gaping, toothless mouth. The eyes looked up at him as if they were real. He squeezed his thumb against the finger and the mouth shut.

Barney laughed to himself. He looked around to

see whether anyone else had noticed what he was doing, but they were all working on their problems. Mrs. Bemouth was busy correcting papers.

Barney leaned across the aisle and poked Jeff, the boy who sat next to him. When Jeff looked up, Barney pointed to the face he had drawn on his hand.

"Hi! My name is Hermie," Barney made the face say, talking out of the side of his own mouth.

Jeff giggled.

"Do you know where I can find a mathematical genius?" the little face seemed to ask. "I need help!"

"Barnett and Jeffrey! Back to your work, please."

Mrs. Bemouth was looking right at Barney. She insisted on calling him by his real name, Barnett.

Barney went back to the problems he was doing over. He tried the second one. "Seven times five is . . ." he couldn't remember. He counted on his fingers, "Five, ten, fifteen, twenty, twenty-five, thirty, thirty-five," But that's what he had written the first time. Why had he erased it? He looked back at his left hand. The little face seemed to be smiling encouragement at him. But he wasn't in a smiling mood himself.

Mrs. Bemouth got up from her desk and started around the room, handing back the math papers they had worked on last Friday. If Barney had made any mistakes on his, he would have to do the problems over at recess.

His heart almost stopped when the teacher laid the paper on his desk. "Oh, no," Barney groaned softly. The workbook page was slashed with red X's, one next to *every* math problem.

Marybeth, who sat in front of him, turned in her seat to check how he'd done. She was a real pain. She always had to be sure she had gotten the best grade in the class. When Marybeth saw all the red marks, she gasped, pulling in her lower lip with her teeth.

Barney hastily tried to cover the page with his hands. "Turn around, nosy," he said.

Then Barney became aware that Mrs. Bemouth was still standing next to his desk. He looked up at her quickly and then down at his paper again.

"Well, Barnett, what happened here?" Mrs. Bemouth asked, nodding toward the workbook paper with the errors marked in red.

"I don't know," he mumbled.

"The carrying is wrong on every single one."

"I guess I forgot how to do it," said Barney miserably.

The two thin perfect curves that Mrs. Bemouth

drew on her face for eyebrows rose as if he had of-
fended her personally. "But we went over it twice last
week," she said.

"I get mixed up," Barney explained.

"That's because you are not paying attention to your
work. Go to the washroom and wash that face off
your hand."

Barney rose from his seat. He covered the Hermie
with his other hand. Curious eyes followed him down
the long aisle to the classroom door. His ears burned
with shame. Nothing like this had ever happened to
him before he came to Hillside.

4

What Hit Me?

After lunch Barney looked for Jeff. If he could choose one person in his class for a friend, it would be him.

Jeff was with a group of mostly older boys playing a game they called foursquare. Barney hung around awhile watching, but no one asked him to join. It was just as well, Barney thought. He had never played the game before, so he probably wouldn't be good at it anyway.

Then Barney saw the boy with the purple and gold jacket standing by the playground fence with his friend, Caruso. They were looking at him and whispering to each other. Barney moved away. He felt more comfortable with as many children between him and the two of them as possible.

He drifted to the part of the schoolyard where the little kids were playing on the slides. Barney had always liked slides. He wished they had a really big one here.

He climbed the ladder of the highest slide. When he had almost reached the last rung, his foot pulled out of its boot. Something was holding it to the step. He stopped climbing and looked behind him. The kid with the purple jacket was squinting up at him. Barney wiggled the boot back on.

"Come on. Come on. Let's go!" the boy said. "You're holding up the line."

Barney sat on the top of the slide, ready to push off, but he kept looking nervously behind him to make sure the boy wasn't up to something else.

"What's the matter? Need a little help?" the boy asked.

"No!"-Barney answered quickly, but he wished he could have thought of something really wise to answer back.

Barney took a deep breath and let himself go, lifting his feet so the rubber soles of his boots wouldn't hold him back. He was halfway down when some-

one's feet hit him in the back with a tooth-jarring thud. Together they slid to the bottom, where Barney pitched forward on his face with the other boy's full weight landing on top of him.

Barney was pinned to the ground until the boy got off him. Then he sat up. His nose felt numb. He explored it with his fingers and was surprised when a lot of blood came off on his hand. Seeing so much of his own blood panicked him and he began to cry.

"I'll get the teacher," a girl said. She ran off with her two friends to be the first to tell the teacher on playground duty. A crowd of curious and excited children began to form around Barney.

"Lenny Coots gave him a bloody nose," someone explained to a newcomer.

That was the first time Barney had heard the boy's name — Lenny, Lenny Coots.

A teacher hurried over with the three girls. "What happened?" he demanded.

"I was going down the slide . . ." Barney took a gulp of air. "And *he* . . ." Barney pointed at Lenny with one hand. The other, the one with blood on it, dangled in front of him as if it, too, were wounded. "He came down right on top of me . . ." Barney had to gulp another breath of air. "And he knocked me on the ground and hit my no-ose!"

The last word ended on a howl.

"I didn't do it on purpose," Lenny protested. "It was an accident, honest. He stopped in the middle of the slide when I was coming down. I couldn't help running into him."

"I think you're too big to be playing on the slides, Coots," the teacher said. "From now on, keep to the other side of the playground."

The teacher helped Barney to his feet. A string of children followed them across the playground as if Barney were the Pied Piper, until the teacher took him inside to the nurse's office.

The nurse gave him some ice to press under his nose, which only made it hurt more. "Will your mother be home?" she asked.

Barney shook his head no and winced because it made his nose hurt. "My mother is at work."

"Then it would be better for you to go back to your classroom," the nurse told him. "Your nose looks much worse than it really is with all that blood. It will stop in a minute."

And it did stop. Barney went to the bathroom to

wash up. He looked in the mirror. There were dried crusts of blood in his nostrils. And his eyes under the wisps of wet hair were as pink from crying as his nose. He looked like some pitiful giant rabbit, and he felt like one, too.

Barney went back to his empty classroom and sat at his desk. The other children started coming in from the playground.

"What's happened to your nose?" asked Cara, who was Marybeth's best friend.

"My brother was hit in the nose and he had to get three stitches," sniffed Marybeth.

"Does it hurt?" Jeff asked.

Barney noticed that most of the Hermie face was still on his hand. The ballpoint ink hadn't washed off. In a voice somewhere between Donald Duck's and Popeye's gruff voice, he made the Hermie say out of the corner of his mouth, "Aw, it's okay. You shoulda seen the *other* guy."

Jeffrey grinned. "Who hit you?" he asked.

"That's what I keep askin'. What hit me?" answered Hermie.

The other kids, who hadn't seen Hermie before, crowded around Barney.

"All I know," Hermie said, encouraged by their laughter, "is dis Lenny Coots kid better watch out, 'cause *I'm* gonna lower da boom on him."

Mrs. Bemouth came in and shut the classroom door. "Lunchtime is over, children. Please take your seats," she announced in her loud voice.

"Mrs. Bigmouth," Jeff said. He jerked his head toward the teacher, who was putting on a smock to protect her dress from the chalk dust.

Barney giggled. He hadn't heard her called that before. It really fit.

"Barnett, I heard you were hurt on the playground. Do you feel all right now?" Mrs. Bemouth asked.

All heads turned toward Barney for the second time that day. But now the eyes were not just curious. They were friendly.

"Barnett feels peachy dandy," the gruff voice of Hermie answered.

5

The Hero

As Barney walked home after school, he was wishing his mother would be there. His nose still felt tender, and he was tired and let down after the excitement.

A snowball whacked him in the back of his head. It was so sudden he didn't realize at first what had happened.

"Did the nursey kiss your nose and make it better?" a sneering voice called from the little country cemetery next to the schoolyard.

Barney felt a knot tighten in his stomach. No, not *him* again. Why couldn't that Coots kid leave him alone?

Lenny bent over to make a second snowball. Barney dropped his lunchbox and scooped up two handfuls of snow. He hastily packed it into a ball and threw wildly at Lenny. He missed him by a mile. He scooped up some more snow and formed another ball.

Lenny threw his snowball at Barney's head. Barney ducked to protect his tender nose, and the snowball clipped his ear. Still in a crouching position, Barney fired off his second ball. It arced toward the ground and Lenny skipped over it, jeering.

That did it for Barney. He was no match for Lenny. He picked up his lunchbox and started walking again, but a little faster. Each step jarred his nose. Then a snowball hit his shoulder with greater force than the last two. Lenny was gaining on him. Barney started running. His lunchbox jangled noisily in his hand. The pain in his nose spread up between his eyes.

There was a woman ahead, holding a little child by the hand. She was waiting to cross the street. Barney ran up and stood next to her as if they were together. Coots wouldn't dare throw any more snowballs now.

The woman crossed the street and Barney was able to walk all the way home with her. The little child kept looking up at him, but the woman pulled it along. When Barney got to his driveway he glanced back, but Lenny Coots had disappeared.

The house was empty. This must be one of the days Russ rode home on the school bus with a boy in his class who lived out on Route 4. It wasn't until dinnertime, when his mother came home with Russ, that Barney could tell them about Lenny and what had happened to his nose.

"I know that little crud!" said Russ. "He's the one who's always coming up to me and making some dumb remark like 'You can't get me,' and then he runs away. What a jerk!"

"Have you told your teacher?" his mother asked Barney.

"I told the playground teacher. But telling my own teacher wouldn't do any good. No one can stop Lenny from getting me on the way home."

Barney's mother sighed. "Well, maybe I'd better call the principal tomorrow. *He* can do something about it."

"No!" cried Barney. "Then Lenny will *really* have it in for me."

His mother studied him for a moment. "Barney . . ."

He looked up at her unhappily.

"Maybe the boy bothers you because you overreact. Maybe he wouldn't pick on you if you didn't make it so much fun for him."

"Yeah," Russ agreed. "You're always blowing a gasket if someone just touches you."

"Sure!" Barney said. "How would *you* like it if someone gave *you* a bloody nose and waited for *you* after school!" At least, Barney thought, his own mother and brother should be on his side.

"You're not going to cry now, are you?" asked Russ.

Barney didn't answer, but his lower lip trembled.

"Aw, c'mon. Don't be such a baby," Russ said with disgust.

"It's all right for you to say 'Don't be a baby.' You're older than Lenny," Barney said angrily.

"Tsss!" Russ hissed with scorn.

"All right. All right, Russ. That's enough," their mother said. She smoothed the hair back from Barney's forehead. "I hate to say this, Barney," she said gently, "but maybe Russ is right. I'm afraid a time comes when you have to stand up for yourself."

"But Lenny's twice as big as me!" Barney wailed.

"Twice my eye!" Russ scoffed.

"Russ!" His mother frowned at him. "Barney, bullies are always cowards at heart. That's why they pick on someone smaller. This boy won't continue to bother you if he knows you'll fight back. He'd rather pick on someone who won't give him any trouble."

"Oh, sure, that's what *you* say." Barney jumped to his feet. "If I try to fight back, I'll just give Lenny an excuse to beat me to a pulp. I hope you'll both be satisfied then!"

Now Barney did begin to cry. "That's why I didn't tell you the first time he picked on me, when he took my sled. I knew neither of you would understand!"

Barney ran up to his room and slammed the door. They could hear his bed slide against the wall as he threw himself on it.

"Boy!" groaned Russ. "He's really hopeless."

"I can't say you were much help," his mother said.

Barney lay face down on the bed and thought about school. What would Jeff do if Lenny picked on him? But Lenny would never bother someone like Jeff. Everyone liked Jeff. Anyway, if he did, Jeff would probably punch him out.

He wished his mother had never made them come here. If they hadn't left their old home, he could still see his father sometimes. *Dad* would help him.

That gave Barney an idea. He looked under the

socks in his top drawer for the piece of paper. His father had given him his telephone number to call if he ever needed anything. He opened the scrap of paper. He felt comforted already, just seeing his dad's neat printing.

Carefully, Barney dialed o for operator, three numbers for the area code back where they used to live, and then his father's number.

"Operator," a metallic voice said.

"What? Oh. I want to call Mel Windsor, collect. I'm Barney Windsor."

Barney could hear ringing and then his father's voice. "Hello?"

"Will you accept a collect call from Barney —"

"I sure will!" his father interrupted.

"Can I talk yet?" Barney asked.

"Hi, sport! How are you?"

It sure felt good to hear his father's voice. Barney was surprised that he sounded so close. He could feel a lump growing in his throat. "I'm okay."

"How's your mom and Russ?"

"They're okay."

"Well, I'm glad to hear that."

There was a pause because Barney didn't know how to start.

"How's your new school?" his father asked.

"It's okay," he said reluctantly. "Well, that's the thing. There's this kid who keeps on picking on me all the time, and I don't know how to make him stop."

"Bop him one!" his father said right off. But then he asked, "How big is he?"

"Lots bigger," Barney answered.

"Hmmm. That makes it sticky, doesn't it? You know, you just reminded me. When I was about your age, there was this kid who scared the pants off me. He kept waiting for me on the way to school. I even pretended I was sick once so I wouldn't have to go."

"So what happened?" Barney asked hopefully.

"I don't remember. He probably got bored with it all and found something else to do."

"Oh." Barney was disappointed.

There was a long pause, and then his father said, "Look, sport, I wish I could give you an answer to your problem. But no one can tell you how you should solve it. You have to work it out your own way." There was another pause. "I'm sure you can handle it. Let me know how you do. Will you?"

Barney nodded silently.

"Say hello to your mom and Russ for me."

"Okay, Dad."

"Bye, sport."

"Bye, Dad."

It was a good thing his dad had hung up because the lump in Barney's throat had grown too big to talk anymore.

The house was cold. Barney got into his pajamas and crawled under the covers. He wondered whether Lenny would be waiting for him again tomorrow. He could see himself crossing the playground in the morning. Suddenly his lunchbox was snatched out of his hand.

"Hey!" he yelled and spun around.

Lenny Coots was opening the box and looking inside. "Oh, boy, brownies! My favorite," he said. He tossed a package to his friend, Caruso. "Here, have some carrot sticks."

Caruso flubbed the catch, and the carrots in their plastic wrapping fell on the ground.

"Tsk, tsk, clumsy," Lenny pretended to scold.

Rolling over on his back, Barney imagined what would happen next. Without warning he swiftly hooked his leg behind Lenny's knee. At the same time he shoved against Lenny's shoulder, flipping him backward.

At this point Jeff and some of his friends came over. "Get'm Barney!" Jeff urged.

Lenny was tall for a sixth-grader, and he hit the ground hard. Before he could get to his feet, Barney applied his submission hold. He grabbed Lenny's wrist with one hand and Lenny's elbow with the other, bending his arm behind his back in a hammerlock.

"Put the lunch back in the box," he said firmly, giving Lenny's wrist a slight jerk, which made him howl.

Now a small crowd gathered to see Lenny get what he deserved. They cheered Barney on as he made Lenny meekly put the brownies in the lunchbox. Then he forced him to crawl to where the carrots lay. Lenny wiped the dirt off the package with his purple jacket.

"Now give it to me," Barney commanded.

"Okay, okay!" Lenny said. "We weren't gonna keep it. We were just kidding around."

Jeff came over to him and said, "Hey, Barney, we're playing foursquare at recess. Will you be on my team?"

Barney turned over in bed and smiled dreamily to himself. Wouldn't it be great if he could take care of Lenny that easily? But things like that only happened in stories. He knew he could never really do it in a million years.

6

Trouble with
Mrs. Bemouth

The next morning Barney left late for school. If he could manage to get there just before the bell rang, he might avoid Lenny. As he hurried across the playground, he saw that everyone had gone inside already.

Just as the outside door slammed behind him, the late bell rang. His classroom was only the second one down the hall. Maybe Mrs. Bemouth wouldn't mark him late. He opened the door very quietly, hoping he would not be noticed.

Mrs. Bemouth was busy putting on the comfortable old shoes she wore during school time. She looked up as Barney slipped into his seat. "You're late,

Barnett," she said. "Two more times and I'll have to send you to the principal's office."

She noticed everything.

Jeff leaned toward him and whispered, "Hey, would you show me that thing with your hand again?"

Even though Barney was flushed from running, he turned an even deeper shade of pink, this time from pleasure. "You mean Hermie?" he asked. "Sure."

Barney drew a better face than the first one, with hair and ears and a big nose.

"Hi, Jeff," he made Hermie say in a small voice. "Did you want to see me?"

Jeff grinned. "Hey, that's great!" he said.

After taking attendance, Mrs. Bemouth asked Cara to pass out the *Weekly Newsletter,* a newspaper that the class subscribed to.

"Children, let's look at the article on page one called 'Thar She Blows!'" the teacher said. "Mark, will you read aloud, please?"

Mark was a quiet boy who sat in the back of the room. He began to read in a dull, expressionless voice about some class that visited an old whaling ship. When he came to the end of the first column, Mrs. Bemouth called on the girl in front of him.

The girl stumbled over so many of the words that

it was hard for Barney to follow in his own copy. He couldn't stop himself from reading ahead about the old whaling days. He was a good reader, and it was like torture to go so slowly. By the time Cara was called upon to read in her rapid, singsong, Barney had finished the story.

There was still another row of readers to go before Mrs. Bemouth would be calling on him. He turned to the back page to do one of the puzzles, but there weren't any this week. What a gyp! He yawned and looked out of the window. A crow was pecking at something in the schoolyard.

Next to Barney, Jeff was doodling in the margin of his newspaper. That reminded Barney of the face he had drawn on his hand. It was the best one he had made so far. He stared at Jeff to get his attention. When Jeff looked up, Barney held up his left hand and made Hermie's face move.

Jeff smiled and signaled Barney to wait a minute. He began to draw a Hermie on his own hand with a green marker. When he finished, he tried to make its jaw move, but he was still awkward at it.

Barney showed Jeff how to make Hermie look as if his false teeth were out, his surprised look, his mean and then his furious look. When Jeff saw Barney's

Hermie with its angry jaw jutting out, he forgot himself and snickered.

"Barnett!"

Mrs. Bemouth was calling on him. Barney looked down at his newspaper in panic. He didn't know what page they were on now. His face started to burn.

"A-a-ah," he said, stalling for time.

Wait, he thought. Marybeth should come before he did. Had she been called on?

"It isn't my turn," he said. "Is it?" He wasn't really sure.

Mrs. Bemouth put her fingertips under her glasses and rubbed her eyes. Then she folded her hands on the desk and blinked at him like an owl with her large magnified eyes. "Barnett, you have not been paying attention. I want you and Jeffrey to stay in at recess."

"I didn't do anything!" Jeff said. But Mrs. Bemouth must have trusted her own opinions about that because she just smiled at the girl sitting behind Barney and signaled for her to begin reading aloud.

After the girl had read a few sentences, Barney stole a look at Jeff. Jeff made an evil face in the direction of Mrs. Bemouth and then smiled at him. Good, thought Barney, feeling relieved. He isn't mad at me for getting him into trouble. Staying in at recess wouldn't be so awful. At least it gave him something to share with Jeff. And besides, all his time in the playground would be spent avoiding Lenny.

But when recess came and the others all happily dressed for the outdoors, Barney became more anxious. Would he and Jeff just be kept inside or would there be some other punishment? Maybe they would be sent to the principal's office.

The room sounded empty and quiet, except for Mrs. Bemouth erasing the blackboard. When she finished, she removed two sheets of paper from a box on her desk and came down the aisle. Barney took a deep breath. Here it comes, he thought to himself. She laid a sheet of paper on each of their desks.

"I want you to complete these sentences on your paper," she said, writing on the blackboard. "When you finish, you may go outside."

Barney copied the first sentence. WHAT I DID WAS WRONG BECAUSE . . . He thought about it for a moment and then wrote, I SHOULD PAY ATTENTION. That was easy.

Then he copied the second sentence. I DID IT BECAUSE . . . Why did he do it? He did it because it was boring to hear people read aloud when he could do it better by himself. He looked at his Hermie. He did it because Hermie was cute and Jeff liked it. It seemed to be the only thing that Jeff did like about him. At last Barney picked up his pencil again and wrote, I DID IT BECAUSE I WAS HAVING FUN WITH MY FRIEND.

After recess Mrs. Bemouth returned the corrected math workbooks from the day before. As she came down the aisle, Barney stared at the desk, feeling hopeless. He had stayed in at recess yesterday to redo the problems that were marked wrong. Mrs. Bemouth had told him to take whatever new work he had not completed and finish it at home. But he had forgotten it.

Sticking out of the workbook that Mrs. Bemouth laid on his desk was a piece of folded paper. "Give this note to your mother," Mrs. Bemouth said. "I want her to come in so we can have a talk about your work."

Barney opened his mouth to object, but then he decided against it. It was no use. Mrs. Bemouth had it in for him. He flipped open his book to where the note marked the last page he had worked on. As usual, it was covered with angry looking red X's. At the top of the page were the words *Messy* and *Incomplete*. At the bottom was written *"Show this page to your mother."*

Marybeth stole a quick peek at him over her shoulder, but when she saw the way he looked at her, she spun around again. Barney focused all the rage he felt at the back of Marybeth's neat head. He would not have been surprised if her curls had begun to smoke from the heat of his glare.

For the rest of the school day the note was on Barney's mind. He dreaded showing it to his mother. Everything he did lately was somehow wrong. She seemed angry at him for just being alive.

He might be having a good time by himself, drawing or something, and she would say, "It's such a nice day. Why are you cooped up in here?" Then she'd tell him to go outside and play in the fresh air like Russ, who was dribbling his basketball.

His mother had gotten a new job in a Hillside real estate office, and it meant she would have to work on Saturdays. When Barney complained that now they would never do any of the things she had promised when they moved to the country, she really lost her temper.

"I'm doing the best I can," she had said. "What do you want from me?"

Well, what did she want from him?

*

On the way home from school, Barney saw Russ with three of his friends. Now that Barney's mother was working, she worried about leaving him home alone every day. She made Russ come home from school at least three days a week to keep him company. That made Russ angry, so he spent the whole time shooting baskets at the hoop on the garage. It was no fun for Barney. His brother's arms were longer, and he was so much better at basketball.

"You just gotta practice. That's all," Russ said.

Barney could practice for the rest of his life, but he still wouldn't be as good as his brother. Besides, he decided, he didn't like basketball anyway.

Barney hurried to catch up with Russ. If Lenny was waiting to ambush him along the way, he wouldn't bother him if he was with his brother.

But the older boys didn't want him tagging along, and Barney was ashamed to tell Russ that he was still afraid of Lenny.

To get rid of Barney, the boys started teasing. One of them, whose name was Gary, said, "Hey Barney, your epidermis is showing."

Barney didn't know what that meant, so he ignored him.

"What didya say? Didya say it was?" asked Gary.

"No," Barney answered.

"Barney says his epidermis isn't showing. His *skin* isn't showing!" Gary shouted with glee.

They all laughed, including Russ, at Gary's great wit. But Barney tried to take it good-naturedly. Russ's friends were almost as bad as Lenny — but not quite.

Barney's mother was lying under a quilt on the living room couch when he got home. She had left work early because she was coming down with a bad cold. Barney fished the note from Mrs. Bemouth out of his pocket and gave it to her.

"Oh, Barney," she said, looking distressed after she read it. "What's this all about?"

Barney shrugged.

"You don't know? Your teacher wants me to take time off from work to see her, and you don't even know why?"

"I don't want to talk about it," Barney muttered.

His mother looked back at the note. "She says that you're not able to keep up in math and you don't pay attention in class."

"That's not true," Barney protested. "I pay attention, but she goes too fast sometimes. She expects me to get everything right away."

"Oh, dear," his mother said. "Maybe she could give you work to do at home. I don't think I learned to do math the same way that you do it, but Russ could probably help you."

Outside, a basketball tapped on the driveway, then there was a slam as it hit the backboard. Russ and his friends all shouted at once. Barney felt a hot wave of resentment toward his brother.

His mother sighed one of her downhearted sighs. "I'll have to see if my boss will let me leave early again tomorrow," she said. But to Barney the expression on her face was saying "Do you have to give me one more thing to worry about?"

Barney scuffed up the nap in the rug with his toe. He didn't know what to say to his mother, and he felt uncomfortable standing there.

His mother sank down on the couch again and shut her eyes. Then she groaned. "I forgot to pick up something for dinner. Would you please take a package of hamburger out of the freezer for us?"

"Sure," Barney said. He was grateful for an excuse to leave the room, and relieved to have something he could do for her.

7

Starting Over

When Barney's class was dismissed the next afternoon, he wanted to be the first one out the door. His mother had said she would call the school if she could come in for a talk with his teacher.

By the end of the day, Barney was still in suspense. And Mrs. Bemouth wouldn't let the class leave until everyone was quiet and the room was cleaned up. Each time the bustling crowd in the hall bumped against the door, Barney thought his mother had come.

At last Mrs. Bemouth let them go. Barney struggled into his coat and ran out without buttoning it. His scarf hung out of his pocket and dragged on the floor. As he pushed through the crowd of noisy children who all seemed to be going the other way, he felt a jerk on his pocket. He clapped his hand against his side. His scarf was gone. Barney looked down the hall. The familiar purple jacket was disappearing around a corner.

Barney followed Lenny to a short hallway where the only door used by the students was the boys' bathroom. He ran in just as one of the doors to the toilet stalls slammed shut. He heard the click of the lock.

Barney pounded on the door of the stall. "Come on, Lenny! Give me my scarf," he shouted. "Give it back or I'm going to the principal's office!"

"La, la la, la," he heard Lenny sing as he sloshed something up and down in the toilet. Barney dropped to his knees and peered under the door. Lenny was dunking his scarf in the water.

"Stop that, Lenny!" Barney started to squeeze under the door. The floor was filthy, and now it was wet from the dripping scarf.

"What's going on here?" boomed a deep voice.

It startled Barney so that he whacked his spine on the bottom of the metal door. He backed out and looked up at one of Russ's junior high teachers from the second floor, the same one who had taken him to the nurse's office when he had bloodied his nose.

"School's over, you two. It's time to go home," the teacher said.

"He's got my scarf," Barney complained, pointing at the locked door.

"Who's in there?" called the teacher.

"Lenny," answered Barney. "Lenny Coots."

"Come out of there, Coots," said the teacher.

The only answer was the toilet flushing.

Barney felt as though his heart had dropped down the drain with the rushing water. His mother would have a fit. She had spent hours making that scarf for him. It was the first thing she had knitted, and she had ripped out part of it twice before it was perfect.

Then the door opened. Lenny stood there wearing a blank look.

"Where's this kid's scarf?" the teacher demanded.

"I just hadda go to the bathroom," Lenny said.

"Liar!" Barney shouted. He turned to the teacher. "He ran in there with my scarf. I saw him."

"I don't have no scarf," Lenny said with a shrug.

"*Now* you don't," Barney said, and he managed to keep his voice from getting quavery, "because you flushed it down."

"Believe me, I don't have his scarf," Lenny insisted.

"There it is!" Barney pointed to the floor of the

next stall where the scarf lay in a sodden mass. "He threw it there," Barney said. "I know he did."

"Pick it up, Lenny," said the teacher.

"But I didn't put it there," Lenny protested.

"Pick it up, Lenny, and put it in the sink. Now!"

"Oh, all right," Lenny grumbled, and he picked up the dripping scarf with two fingers and dropped it in the sink.

"Now wring it out."

"Whaddaya mean?" Lenny asked.

"Squeeze all the water out," the teacher said patiently, "and then wrap it in some paper towels."

Lenny followed the teacher's directions, his nose wrinkled in disgust. When he finished, he left the untidy bundle on the sink as if handing it back to Barney was too much for his pride.

"Okay," the teacher said. "Out of here, both of you. And Coots, if I see you hanging around after school anymore, you're in trouble. You know what I mean?"

Lenny nodded.

The teacher pointed to the door. "Now, out!"

Lenny left in a hurry.

Barney picked up the scarf in the paper towels. "Thank you," he said.

The teacher nodded.

As Barney hurried by his classroom, he saw Mrs. Bemouth at her desk. She was talking to his mother. He got past the open door without being seen.

All the way home Barney expected the figure in the purple jacket to be waiting for him somewhere, but Lenny never appeared.

In the kitchen, Russ was slicing cheese and stacking it to match a pile of crackers. He cleaned out half the contents of the refrigerator every day after school.

"Hi. What you got there?" he asked.

Barney looked down at his soggy package. The wet scarf had leaked through the paper towels, and his hands were freezing cold.

"Lenny took my scarf and tried to flush it down the toilet."

Russ wrinkled his nose. "Gross!"

Barney told his brother how the teacher had come just in time. When he came to the part where Lenny had to wring out the scarf, Russ snickered.

"Yeah, very funny," said Barney.

"Well, it is," Russ said. "I would've liked to have seen old Lenny wrapping it up real nice for you."

"But now he's got an excuse to *really* demolish me!" Barney's voice rose in panic when he thought about meeting up with Lenny the next time.

Russ rolled his eyes upward as if to ask the heavens for aid. He had no patience with such a baby.

Barney read his expression. "I know you think I'm supposed to stand up to Lenny. But there's no way I can win against him, Russ!"

"Okay, okay! Don't get so worked up," Russ said, trying to soothe him. "Take it easy a minute, will you?" He stood tapping the cheese knife against the cutting board, thinking. Barney warmed his stiff hands under his armpits.

"Look," Russ said. "Suppose I meet you in the parking lot after school tomorrow. If Lenny tries anything, we'll fix him. I wouldn't mind having an excuse to squash that little bug."

Barney's face lit up. "Would you?"

Russ put an arm around his brother's skinny shoulders and gave him a rough but friendly shake. "C'mon, cheer up! It's going to be all right. You'll see. Here, have a cracker."

At first Barney wasn't convinced that his brother was really going to help him. But then Russ started joking about how they were going to make mincemeat out of Lenny. He walked around the kitchen floor on his knees to imitate Lenny begging them for mercy.

Barney giggled with delight. This was like the old days when Barney was a little kid and they used to play together all the time — the days before Russ got so far ahead of him in everything.

Suddenly Barney heard a car door slam. His mother was back from her meeting with Mrs. Bemouth. Barney's first thought was to run up to his room, to put off having to talk about his schoolwork. But before he could move, the back door flew open with his mother behind it. Her arms were full of groceries.

"I have to sign up for a real estate course tonight and I'm running late," she announced.

Just before she dumped the bags on the counter, the soggy bottom of one broke and the cans crashed to the floor.

"Barney, would you pick those up?" she asked on her way out to the car again. "Russ, help me. I still have a few more bags."

Barney picked up the cans and put them on the counter. As his mother began to open the paper bags and sort out the groceries, he tried to decide what kind of mood she was in. All he could see was that the dark smudges she had under her eyes lately were even deeper, and her cold had reddened her nose.

Finally, he couldn't wait any longer to hear what

had happened. "Okay, what did she say about me?" he asked.

"Just a minute, I have to get these packages into the freezer or they'll melt."

Barney sat down at the table.

"Your teacher seems like a very nice person," his mother said over her shoulder. She was trying to rearrange the inside of the freezer so she could squeeze in a half-gallon of ice cream.

"Nice to grownups, maybe," Barney said gloomily.

"And she likes you."

Barney made a face. "I'll bet!" he said.

"Really, Barney." His mother came over to the table and took his face between her hands. "Mrs. Be-mouth says —"

"It's pronounced Bi-muth, like in Plymouth," he interrupted.

"Mrs. *Bi*-muth says you're very creative, that you write beautiful stories."

"Then why does she make me do them over all the time?" he asked.

"She thinks that you're a bright boy and you can do better."

"How does *she* know what I can do!" he objected.

"Barney . . ." Looking for help, she turned to Russ,

who was leaning against the doorjamb. He raised his eyebrows and shrugged.

She lifted her hands in a pleading gesture. "Mrs. Bemouth just wants to help you," she said, trying to keep her voice calm. "*I* just want to help you."

"If she just wants to help me, why does she yell? She kills my ears." Barney held his hands over his ears with a pained look.

"Mrs. Bemouth doesn't think you're trying very hard."

"I *am* trying. She expects me to know things I never had before. She keeps picking on me. *Everyone* keeps picking on me. Even you now!"

Barney got up from the table. As he passed Russ, his brother tried to grab his arm, but Barney pulled away and stamped up to his room.

"Barney . . ." his mother whispered.

Had he just drifted off to sleep or had he been asleep for a long time? Barney became aware that his mother was sitting on the edge of his bed. Then he remembered that when he had gone downstairs for dinner, she had already left.

"Is everything okay?" she asked.

"Mmmhmm."

"Did you get anything to eat?"

"Russ fixed me the rest of the spaghetti," he croaked sleepily.

"Barney, everything's going to be all right. I know it's not easy . . . starting over in a new school and making new friends. And I know you were very fond of Debbie. But Mrs. Bemouth is really a nice person. You'll see."

She sat there a minute holding his hand. Her familiar shape blocked the light from the hall.

"Tonight was my first class. I have to get my real estate license so that I can earn more money. It's been a long time since I've had to study. It's hard for *me* to start again, too. I'm a little scared. I don't know if I can go to work and school and do a good job of taking care of you guys, too." She stroked his hair. "You're going to have to help me."

"I will, Mom," Barney promised.

She kissed his cheek and said, "I know you will."

Barney wasn't so sure about Mrs. Bemouth. Still, he was glad his mother had waked him up. He felt himself drifting away into sleep.

"I love you, Barney."

"I love you, too, Mom."

8

Something Special

Barney's best time in school was on Thursday afternoons when they had art. All the desks were pushed together to make one big table that the class could sit around.

On this Thursday Mrs. Bemouth brought out cartons of junk that the children had been collecting for weeks, things like pieces of Styrofoam and tubes from paper towels. With the junk they were going to construct trash art. Mrs. Bemouth passed out glue, scissors, and poster paint and told everyone to go to it.

Barney looked over the heap on the table. He wanted to make something really special. The long egg cartons reminded him of the caterpillars he had made in kindergarten. They used to cut off one row of bumps that held the eggs, and paint the cardboard bright colors with a face on one end.

The Hermie on Barney's hand had given him an idea. There was always a Hermie on Barney's left hand now. Jeff had one, too. And some of the other kids had begun to copy them. Hermies made with markers could last through several hand washings if you were careful.

In both small ends of the carton, Barney cut out a hole large enough for his arm to fit through. He tried it on for size . . . a perfect fit. Then he painted the top of the box with yellow, black, and green stripes. The bumps on the bottom became black feet. He fitted the body of the caterpillar on his left arm like a cast and had Jeff, who was sitting next to him, tape it shut. It looked good, very good.

Barney slid the caterpillar across his desk toward Jeff. The Hermie face became its face. As Barney moved his wrist, the caterpillar seemed to be looking around at the pile of trash.

"Yuk!" it said. "Is this the town dump?"

"Just a minute," said Jeff. "He needs something more."

Jeff searched through the pile until he found one of the paper-covered wire twisties meant to hold a

garbage bag shut. He twisted it once around the base of Barney's middle finger with the ends sticking up.

"Feelers!" squealed Sally, the smallest girl in the class. "That's cute!"

Barney beamed.

"I'm hungry," said the caterpillar in the mellow, musical voice Barney gave him. "I just hatched out of an egg."

"You mean an egg carton," corrected Jeff. The children sitting nearby laughed. They had all stopped working to watch Barney's caterpillar.

"You don't eat apples, do you?" said a snappy voice from the far end of the table. Mrs. Bemouth had cut an apple in half, and she was clapping the two parts together like a wide mouth. Two white thumbtack eyes made the apple look more like a face. The children around the table were delighted. Mrs. Bemouth had never revealed her playful side before.

The caterpillar shook its head seriously. "No, I eat leaves."

"But it's winter. There aren't any leaves now," said the apple.

"Then I'll have a candy bar."

"A candy bar?" said Mrs. Bemouth, forgetting to be the apple. "Caterpillars don't eat candy bars!"

"I do," said the caterpillar. He nodded his head and smiled.

"But candy bars will ruin your teeth," said Mrs. Bemouth, playing her part now as the apple.

"I don't have any teeth," said the caterpillar. "See?" And, sure enough, when the caterpillar opened his mouth, it was as bare of teeth as the palm of Barney's hand.

The entire class, even Mrs. Bemouth, broke up with laughter. Barney had never seen her laugh before. He realized that he had never seen her teeth show. It changed her whole face.

Mrs. Bemouth resumed her usual expression after dabbing her eyes with a tissue. But it was harder to quiet the class. They were all begging to get a close look at Barney's caterpillar.

Mrs. Bemouth's voice rose over the classroom noise. "There are only five minutes left, children. Let's clean up and put our desks back."

She began to assign a job to each of them. "Barnett and Jeffrey," she added, "I want to see you both after school."

Barney was stunned. What had they done now? He looked over at Jeff, who rolled his eyes and made a comic face. It was a mystery to him, too. Whatever it was, Barney hoped his mother wouldn't have to come to school again.

Barney and Jeff waited at their desks while all but a few stragglers left. Why can't they hurry up! Barney thought, impatient to get this over with.

Mrs. Bemouth was packing a tote bag with papers to mark, and tidying the top of her desk. At last she took a pack of cards from a desk drawer and came down the aisle. In the empty room Barney could hear the floorboards creak under her tread.

Mrs. Bemouth lowered herself heavily onto Marybeth's empty desk and faced them. "These are flash cards," she said. "Maybe you've seen them before."

Both Barney and Jeff nodded. In Barney's old school they had used flash cards as a math game to practice addition and subtraction.

"A lot of your trouble, Barney, is that you're in a different place in math than the rest of us. I was hoping you'd be able to catch up. But you're not sure of your times tables, are you?"

Barney shook his head.

"For the next week or so, when the class is busy with math workbooks, I want you and Jeffrey to go in the quiet corner and work with these cards. Take turns. Jeffrey, you can use a little polishing on your times tables, too. All set?"

Barney and Jeff exchanged grins and nodded. They were going to get out of doing those rotten workbooks for a while. This would be more like fun.

Mrs. Bemouth slapped her thighs. "Let's go home," she said.

George Mars, one of Jeff's friends, was waiting for him outside the classroom door, and they went home together. Someone was always waiting for Jeff. But Barney didn't mind so much this time. He was going to have Jeff all to himself at least part of every day. He couldn't wait for tomorrow to start working with the cards.

9

Russ to the Rescue

Barney had already crossed the playground before he remembered Russ was going to meet him in the parking lot. So much had happened that afternoon.

He looked back. Only one girl was there, taking her bike out of the almost empty rack. On the playground a few kids had stayed to climb on the monkey bars. Either Russ had waited for a while and then gone home or he'd forgotten about his promise. Probably he'd found something better to do.

Barney started home, hurrying past the old cemetery next to the schoolyard. He had just started to relax, thinking that today he would make it without any trouble, when he was startled by a loud siren behind him. Barney turned. Lenny Coots was speeding toward him on a bicycle.

It was too late to get out of the way. Lenny passed so close that the handlebars brushed against Barney's arm. Lenny bumped off the curb into the street and circled behind Barney. Making a wheelie, Lenny lifted the front wheel over the curb and rode up on the sidewalk again.

Barney decided not to pay any attention to him. Lenny wouldn't *dare* to run him down. If Barney ignored him, maybe Lenny would get bored and go away. He kept on walking.

This time the bicycle did not race past. Wobbling crazily, Lenny slowed to Barney's pace and began to bump the back of his legs.

Barney broke into a run. He zigzagged in an attempt to avoid Lenny's front wheel. "Stop! Stop, will you?" he cried. "It's not funny!"

But Lenny continued his attack, roaring like a racing engine.

Barney looked around desperately for help. Then he saw his escape route — the fence, the wooden cemetery fence. He threw his lunchbox and the cardboard caterpillar over it. Then, like a rabbit being chased by the hounds, he slipped between the rails.

The wind picked up the caterpillar and carried it away over the icy surface of the snow, but Barney didn't notice.

Barney's right hand was still gripping the lower rail when Lenny rammed into it, pinching his fingers between the tire and the fence. Barney was so relieved to get the fence between himself and Lenny that he took no notice of the painfully scraped fingers. He quickly snatched up the lunchbox, forgetting the caterpillar he was so proud of.

Barney started to run along the edge of the cemetery. But what would he do when he got to the corner? Unless he wanted to spend the night there, he would have to cross the street. Then there would be no way to avoid Lenny unless someone came along whom he could hide behind.

By the time Barney reached the corner of the fence, Lenny was already down the next block. As Barney watched, he disappeared around a curve in the road. Barney ducked under the fence and ran across the street. Maybe Lenny had gotten tired of the game by now.

When Barney came to the same curve, he walked way out in the road to see if Lenny was waiting out of sight. There was no sign of him. Barney sighed with relief. Four more blocks to go and he'd be home.

Barney made a run for it. He had covered the first two blocks when Lenny returned. Like a large, graceful bird of prey he swooped from one side of the road to the other, riding no-hands.

Once again Lenny rode past and circled behind Barney. Barney walked backward, warily watching to see what Lenny was up to this time. Lenny started the racing engine sound and drove straight at him.

Barney knew he wouldn't be able to outrun the bicycle, so he dropped his lunchbox and held his arms out to protect his body. Just before the bicycle hit, he grabbed for the handlebars. At the same time he flinched, shutting his eyes and turning his head away.

Then two surprising things happened. Barney was standing braced to meet the shock when he heard the skid of tires and the clatter of a falling bicycle. At the last minute Lenny had swerved to avoid hitting him and skidded on sand left on an icy patch of road by the highway department.

As Lenny went down, Barney heard a familiar voice yell, "Hey, stupid! Maybe I'd better teach you how to ride a bike."

It was Russ. He hadn't forgotten. Barney had never been so glad to see his brother.

Lenny scrambled to his feet and got back on his bike. He obviously didn't want to learn any lessons from Russ. Russ had almost caught up with them, so Lenny didn't get much of a head start. Russ kept up with him on foot all the way down the block. Barney jumped up and down with glee, seeing Lenny pedal for dear life.

When Barney got to the front of their house, Russ was trotting back from the opposite direction.

"Did you get him?" Barney yelled.

"Nah. I scared him plenty, though."

"What're you doin' that for, sonny?" Mr. Greybar called from across the street. "A big kid like you should find someone your own size to pick on."

Mr. Greybar was retired from his job with the telephone company. He spent all his time now taking care of his little house, painting the wood trim and keeping the small front yard neat.

"He's picking on *me* all the time," Barney shouted. Why did the old man have to butt in? It wasn't any of his business.

"That's no way to solve things," Mr. Greybar said. "Fightin'. You tell his parents. They'll take care of him."

"They wouldn't believe anything bad about their

little darling," Russ muttered.

"What's that?" Mr. Greybar was a little deaf. Barney's mother said that was why he talked so much. He was lonely, but he couldn't hear what the other person was saying.

"It won't do any good, telling his parents," Russ yelled.

"That's right." Mr. Greybar nodded. "Tell his parents. That's their job, to take care of him," he said as he went into his house.

Russ groaned.

Just then Lenny came riding down the street. He felt he had gotten the best of Russ and now he was looking for more attention. From inside his jacket he pulled out the caterpillar Barney had left behind in the cemetery. He threw it on the ground in front of their house. As he passed them he stood up on the pedals and pumped harder.

"I'm going to get that little turd!" Russ swore and took off after him.

Barney couldn't stand missing the outcome of the chase. He ran down to the corner, but Lenny and Russ had disappeared from sight.

Barney headed back home. Even though the sun set early this time of year, he shivered more with excitement than from the cold. When he looked up, he was disappointed to see Lenny riding toward him. He had made it around the block again.

Russ was still keeping up with Lenny, but he was puffing hard. It was clear that he would soon be left behind. Lenny was enjoying the game too much to quit, so he slowed a little to encourage Russ to keep on running. That enabled Russ to get close enough to grab Lenny's back fender. It jerked out of his hand, though, and he stumbled and fell.

Barney held his breath, hopefully, as the bicycle wobbled for a second. But then Lenny regained his balance.

Russ got to his feet right away, but it was obvious that he had run out of steam. All he could do was bend over and gasp for air, his hands braced on his knees. His face was bright red and he sounded as if he were going to throw up.

Barney was so concerned for his brother that he almost missed what happened next. As Lenny rode away, looking back over his shoulder and jeering at them, he didn't see the car coming around the corner.

Barney and Russ were startled by the scream of tires as their mother slammed her foot on the brake. She had been hurrying home from work and didn't see Lenny sooner because of the hedge around the corner lot.

Her car skidded across the street. It rocked to a stop as the sides of the wheels hit the curb. Lenny ran into the side of it. For an instant both Barney, Russ, and their mother were paralyzed with shock. Then she opened the door and ran around to the other side of the car.

"Oh, no!" She held her hands up to her mouth in horror when she saw the boy and his bicycle on the ground. But as Lenny began to untangle himself, she took a deep breath of relief. Barney and Russ stood timidly at the front of the car and watched.

"Are you all right?" their mother asked, pulling the bicycle off of Lenny.

"Yeah," he answered as he gingerly put his weight on a bruised ankle. He took the bicycle and gave it a trial push. The back fender scraped against the tire.

"Here, let me help you," Barney's mother said, and she pulled the fender clear of the back wheel. "Are you sure you're all right? Let me drive you home."

Lenny shook his head. He seemed afraid, not just because of the accident, but of Barney's mother. He got on the bike and rode off in a hurry without looking at any of them. The sound of his pedal hitting the bent chain guard echoed down the darkening street.

Barney's mother leaned against the car with her eyes shut. Her face looked very white against her dark coat, and she held her elbows tightly as if she were trying to keep herself together. Then she opened her eyes and looked at Russ and Barney. They were watching her anxiously.

"How awful! Do you realize I almost killed him?" she said.

"*I'm* going to kill him if I ever catch up with him!" said Russ. He had been scared when Lenny collided with the car, but now his rage came rushing back.

Russ's mother was surprised at his anger. "Isn't he one of your friends?" she asked.

"No, Mom," Barney explained. "That's Coots, the kid I told you about. The one who keeps picking on me. Russ was trying to get back at him."

His mother looked down the empty street as if she wanted to call back the pale, frightened boy and get to the bottom of this. Then, since nothing was going to be solved standing there in the dark, she said, "I'd better move the car."

While she started the car and pulled into the driveway, Barney walked home with Russ. His brother's hand rested lightly below the back of his neck. It made

Barney feel closer to his brother than he had in a long time.

Barney's mashed caterpillar lay in front of their house. Russ picked up what was left of it. "Is this yours?" he asked. "Coots ran over it."

"It's okay. I can make another one," Barney said, taking it. "I was going to show it to you and Mom."

As they came inside and took off their coats, their mother said, "Brr, it's chilly. How about some hot chocolate?"

"Yes!" both brothers agreed.

Barney wrapped the battered egg carton around his arm and held it together with his other hand. "I want my hot chuggle with marshmallow," he said in the caterpillar's voice.

"You used to call it 'chuggle' when you were little," Russ said. "Mom, look what Barney made."

His mother admired the puppet and tried to console Barney over its ruin by adding four marshmallows to his cup of hot chocolate.

Barney was in too good a mood to be upset and stuffed the caterpillar in the garbage can. "After all, he was supposed to be trash art," he said. "Maybe he'll make a cocoon in there."

"And come out a butterfly," added his mother.

10

No More Running

The next day Mrs. Bemouth asked Barney to stay after school for two weeks. But this time it wasn't a punishment. She had chosen him to feed the fish.

His class had a salt-water tank with real fish in it. That is, they hadn't been bought in a pet store. The class had gone on a field trip in the fall and netted some crabs, snails, and several kinds of fish. Lying on the bottom were two curious little creatures, sea cucumbers. They looked like tar balls with hair, buried in the sand.

After everyone had left that afternoon, Barney went to the refrigerator in the janitor's closet and got a chunk of frozen fish. Then he took a special knife from Mrs. Bemouth's desk drawer to shave curls of the frozen flesh into the water. As soon as he stood over their tank, the fish swam to the surface with mouths open and swallowed each bit of food in one gulp.

Barney didn't care if he got home late. There was nothing to do there anyway but look at cartoons on television. The best part about feeding the fish was that Lenny would be gone by the time he finished, so he wouldn't have to worry about meeting him on the way home.

Friday was a cold, gray winter day. The windows of the classroom had steamed up. Barney lingered at the tank, watching the fish search out the last scraps of food. He heard two teachers wishing one another a good weekend and a door slammed somewhere, making a hollow sound through the empty halls. Finally the building grew quiet and the swish of the janitor's broom came nearer. Soon he would be piling chairs on desks in Barney's room and shooing him out.

Barney got his coat. The air smelled stale and the coat closet was sour with forgotten sneakers and dirty sweatshirts. He clumped down the hallway in his rubber boots. Light from the open classroom doors striped the dark floor.

Barney shoved open the heavy outside door. The playground was deserted and the parking lot was almost empty. As he waded through the puddles, Barney broke the reflection of the gray skies. He looked up as a car went by in the street, splashing slush high on both sides. It was then that he saw Lenny waiting for him at the end of the parking lot. He must have found out Barney was staying late. Behind him, on the wall around the playground, a pile of ammunition was lined up. Slushballs.

Barney stopped. His mouth dropped open with surprise, and then his shoulders sagged with a feeling of hopelessness. Lenny grinned, and he let fly the ball he was packing. Barney heard the ball whizz past his cheek and splatter on the pavement behind him. Lenny grabbed another ball and threw it.

Barney held his arms up to protect his head. The snowball hit his shoulder and stuck there. "Cut it out!" he yelled.

"Cut it out!" Lenny mimicked, wrinkling up his face. "Here's one I've been saving just for you."

He selected a slushball from the pile and held it up. It had been packed to an icy hardness. "And it has a present inside," he said.

Russ had told Barney that sometimes kids hid rocks in the center of their snowballs. He turned and ran as fast as he could, back to the school door.

"Why don't you get your brother?" Lenny called. "Chicken! Bu-uk, buk, buk, bu-uk," he crowed.

Barney opened the door and slipped inside. The last snowball skidded along the floor next to him.

He ran up the short flight of steps and rested at the top. There was a thudding beat in his head like running feet. He tried to think of what to do next. He could sneak out the front door, but he would still have to pass Lenny at the parking lot. There was no other way to go home and no Russ to help him now.

Barney sat down on the top step. It was late. Soon it would be time for his mother to come home. Then he could call her up and ask her to come and get him. But the school would be closed. He would be locked inside.

He heard footsteps coming down the flight of stairs above him. He thought everyone had gone home except the janitor.

"Barnett! What are you doing here?" It was Mrs. Bemouth.

"Is something the matter?" Mrs. Bemouth sounded surprisingly kind.

All of a sudden the tears came. Barney couldn't help it. His shoulders shook and his face was pulled down like a tragic mask.

"Why, Barney, what has happened? Tell me."

But Barney couldn't answer. He tried to catch his breath, but his chest heaved with great sobs.

Mrs. Bemouth sat down next to him and enfolded him in her arms. Gradually, Barney brought himself under control and he became aware that the teacher was holding him. She felt very soft and warm under his cheek. And he was surprised at how nice she smelled, something faint and sweet, like flowers. But then he was embarrassed. He pulled away from her and wiped his nose with the sleeve of his jacket.

"Come on," Mrs. Bemouth said, taking his hand. "We'll fix you up."

He trotted obediently behind her. When they got to their classroom, Mrs. Bemouth brought him a cup of water from the sink and gave him a wet paper towel. After wiping his face, Barney felt calmer.

"Now, tell me what's wrong," she said gently.

Barney told her how Lenny had been picking on him every day and how he was waiting for him now, outside.

"You stay here. I'll settle this with that Lenny

Coots," she said with determination. "No one, absolutely no one should be afraid to go home."

Barney felt cheered. This he would love to see. He got a picture in his mind of Mrs. Bemouth bearing down on a trembling Lenny who was begging for mercy. But then he became alarmed.

"Oh, no, don't do that," he pleaded. "It'll just make it worse."

"Well, what would you like me to do?" the teacher asked. "You can't stay here forever. You just tell me what you'd like me to do."

Mrs. Bemouth bent close to him, searching his face with her nearsighted eyes. She must have just put on lipstick, and the grains of fresh powder clinging to her fuzzy skin made her eyes look watery by contrast. But the expression in them was anxious. She really cared about him. Barney swallowed. What could she do? What could anyone do? Oh, why did he have to be such a wimp?

Mrs. Bemouth sat down at her desk and opened the bottom drawer. She made a little grunt each time she bent over to take off a broken-down, comfortable shoe and replace it with one of the shoes in the drawer. Barney noticed that little pads shaped like Life

Savers were stuck on her crooked toes. He looked away quickly.

"Now!" Mrs. Bemouth said, slapping her thighs and standing up as she always did when she meant business. "Would you like me to drive you home in my car?"

Barney imagined himself riding safely past Lenny in Mrs. Bemouth's car. But tomorrow, everyone in school would hear from Lenny how Barney's teacher had to drive him home.

Barney shook his head. "No, thank you."

"Would you feel better if I went as far as the parking lot with you to make sure that Lenny's gone?"

Barney was so tired that he didn't even feel afraid any more. He just wanted to go home.

"It's all right . . . I'll go home by myself," he said.

Barney pushed open the school's outside door. He hadn't taken his coat off, and the cold air felt good after the overheated classroom. He looked around for Lenny, but the parking lot and the playground were empty.

He was halfway down the cemetery block before Lenny came out from hiding behind one of the bushes and climbed over the low fence. He must have thought that Barney was going to bring the principal or someone with him.

Lenny hefted another snowball. "I'll give you ten to get away this time," he said, grinning.

Barney hated that grin. Lenny felt so sure of himself. Barney knew it was because Lenny only picked on a sure thing like him, someone who would run for his life like a scared rabbit. From deep down in his gut, the anger boiled up.

"I'm not running," he said. At first, he only had the courage to croak it hoarsely.

"What'd you say?" Lenny had heard him. He just hadn't expected it.

"I SAID I'M **NOT** RUNNING!" This time it came out louder than Barney meant to say it.

"Oh . . . so you're not running." Lenny put his hands on his hips in a threatening posture. "Then what *are* you going to do?"

What was he going to do? Knock Lenny down the way he had in his superhero daydream? Apply a hammerlock, his submission hold? No. That was just a dream. But he knew one thing; he wasn't going to run anymore.

Lenny stood shifting the snowball between his hands, blocking the way. Instead of trying to get past by stepping into the street, Barney walked up to him. You *can't* cry! You *can't* cry! he told himself. Crying would be giving up. You *can't* give up this time!

"I don't care anymore what you do," Barney said between his teeth. "I'm *not* going to run. You'll have to kill me first, 'cause I'm not going to run away."

He was so close to Lenny that he could see the little chicken pox scar between his eyes, pale eyes that always narrowed when he whispered to his friend Caruso. Barney couldn't see what was in those eyes now. They were hidden behind lowered lids.

Barney was shaking. He shook so hard he had to clench his teeth so they wouldn't rattle. It was pure rage that gave him the nerve to shout, "Well . . . don't you want to knock me down? Don't you want to throw my hat in the mud or something? How are you going to get your kicks this time?"

Lenny snickered, and then quickly stopped himself. He looked over his shoulder and took a deep breath. His face twitched nervously, but he didn't answer.

Then it suddenly struck Barney — he was making Lenny uncomfortable! Lenny hadn't expected him to react this way, and he didn't know how to handle it.

"Well . . . ?" Barney pressed, his confidence building.

Lenny's eyes flicked up for an instant. He grinned, but this time sheepishly. Then he shrugged.

"I don't know what *you're* going to do, but *I'm* going home," Barney said.

As he passed Lenny, he couldn't keep his shoulders from hunching ever so slightly, braced for the blow of that snowball at the back of his head. But the blow never came.

At the last corner before his house, Barney had to stop to let a car pass. He looked back quickly to see if Lenny was following. The sidewalk was empty. He had won this one.

Barney started to cry with relief, and to laugh. Both together. Then he began running, but not away from anyone this time.

He hoped Russ would be home. He couldn't wait to see him, to tell him what had happened. And then he was going to call his father.

√3